Culhwch and Olwen

Anonymous

MythBank

Contents

About MythBank

MythBank is a website devoted to the documentation and study of stories. As part of that initiative, this collection was created with the purpose of ensuring all public domain classics had attractive, uniform, and readily available print copies and ebooks.

Through print on demand, many classics that are lesser-known or have limited runs can still be available for anyone who wants it, keeping the price steady and reducing the need to search the dregs of used books for a copy that might cost ten times what it's worth.

We hope you enjoy this collection of classics and recommend you visit our website to learn more. Additionally, you will find other classics in this collection that are designed to match the same branding and tone of this volume, so they look amazing on your shelf or your device. Check them out!

Part 1

KILYDD THE SON OF Prince Kelyddon desired a wife as a helpmate, and the wife that he chose was Goleuddydd, the daughter of Prince Anlawdd. And after their union, the people put up prayers that they might have an heir. And they had a son through the prayers of the people. From the time of her pregnancy Goleuddydd became wild, and wandered about, without habitation; but when her delivery was at hand, her reason came back to her. Then she went to a mountain where there was a swineherd, keeping a herd of swine. And through fear of the swine the queen was delivered. And the swineherd took the boy, and brought him to the palace; and he was christened, and they called him Kilhwch, because he had been found in a swine's burrow. Nevertheless the boy was of gentle lineage, and cousin unto Arthur; and they put him out to nurse.

After this the boy's mother, Goleuddydd, the daughter of Prince Anlawdd, fell sick. Then she called her husband unto her, and said to him, "Of this sickness I shall die, and thou wilt take another wife. Now wives are the gift of the Lord, but it would be wrong for thee to harm thy son. Therefore I charge thee that thou take not a wife until thou see a briar with two blossoms upon my grave." And this he promised her. Then she besought him to dress her grave every year, that nothing might grow thereon. So the queen died. Now the king sent an attendant every morning to see if anything were growing upon the grave. And at the end of the seventh year the master neglected that which he had promised to the queen.

One day the king went to hunt, and he rode to the place of burial to see the grave, and to know if it were time that he should take a wife; and the king saw the briar. And when he saw it, the king took counsel where he should find a wife. Said one of his counsellors, "I know a wife that will suit thee well, and she is the wife of King Doged." And they resolved to go to seek her; and they slew the king, and brought away his wife and one daughter that she had along with her. And they conquered the king's lands.

On a certain day, as the lady walked abroad, she came to the house of an old crone that dwelt in the town, and that had no tooth in her head. And the queen said to her, "Old woman, tell me that which I shall ask thee, for the love of Heaven. Where are the children of the man who has carried me away by violence?"

Said the crone, "He has not children."

Said the queen, "Woe is me, that I should have come to one who is childless!"

Then said the hag, "Thou needest not lament on account of that, for there is a prediction that he shall have an heir by thee, and by none other. Moreover, be not sorrowful, for he has one son."

The lady returned home with joy; and she asked her consort, "Wherefore hast thou concealed thy children from me?"

The king said, "I will do so no longer." And he sent messengers for his son, and he was brought to the Court.

His stepmother said unto him, "It were well for thee to have a wife, and I have a daughter who is sought of every man of renown in the world."

"I am not yet of an age to wed," answered the youth. Then she said unto him, "I declare to thee, that it is thy destiny not to be suited with a wife until thou obtain Olwen, the daughter of Yspaddaden Penkawr." And the youth blushed, and the love of the maiden diffused itself through all his frame, although he had never seen her. And his father inquired of him, "What has come over thee my son, and what aileth thee?"

"My stepmother has declared to me that I shall never have a wife until I obtain Olwen, the daughter of Yspaddaden Penkawr."

"That will be easy for thee," answered his father. "Arthur is thy cousin. Go, therefore, unto Arthur, to cut thy hair, and ask this of him as a boon."

And the youth pricked forth upon a steed with head dappled grey, of four winters old, firm of limb, with shell-formed hoofs, having a bridle of linked gold on his head, and upon him a saddle of costly gold. And in the youth's hand were two spears of silver, sharp, well-tempered, headed with steel, three ells in length, of an edge to wound the wind, and cause blood to flow, and swifter than the fall of the dewdrop from the blade of reed-grass upon the earth when the dew of June is at the heaviest. A gold-hilted sword was upon his thigh, the blade of which was of gold, bearing a cross of inlaid gold of the hue of the lightning of heaven: his war-horn was of ivory. Before him were two brindled white-breasted greyhounds, having strong collars of rubies about their necks, reaching from the shoulder to the ear. And the one that was on the left side bounded across to the right side, and the one on the right to the left, and like two sea-swallows sported around him. And his courser cast up four sods with his four hoofs, like four swallows in the air, about his head, now above, now below. About him was a four-cornered cloth of purple, and an apple of gold was at each corner, and every one of the apples was of the value of an hundred kine. And there was precious gold of the value of three hundred kine upon his shoes, and upon his stirrups, from his knee to the tip of his toe. And the blade of grass bent not beneath him, so light was his courser's tread as he journeyed towards the gate of Arthur's Palace.

Spoke the youth, "Is there a porter?"

"There is; and if thou holdest not thy peace, small will be thy welcome. I am Arthur's porter every first day of January. And during every other part of the year but this, the office is filled by Huandaw, and Gogigwc, and Llaeskenym, and Pennpingyon, who goes upon his head to save his feet, neither towards the sky nor towards the earth, but like a rolling stone upon the floor of the court."

"Open the portal."

"I will not open it."

"Wherefore not?"

"The knife is in the meat, and the drink is in the horn, and there is revelry in Arthur's hall, and none may enter therein but the son of a king of a privileged country, or a craftsman bringing his craft. But there will be refreshment for thy dogs, and for thy horses; and for thee there will be collops cooked and peppered, and luscious wine and mirthful songs, and food for fifty men shall be brought unto thee in the guest chamber, where the stranger and the sons of other countries eat, who come not unto the precincts of the Palace of Arthur. Thou wilt fare no worse there than thou wouldest with Arthur in the Court. A lady shall smooth thy couch, and shall lull thee with songs; and early to-morrow morning, when the gate is open for the multitude that came hither to-day, for thee shall it be opened first, and thou mayest sit in the place that thou shalt choose in Arthur's Hall, from the upper end to the lower."

Said the youth, "That I will not do. If thou openest the gate, it is well. If thou dost not open it, I will bring disgrace upon thy Lord, and evil report upon thee. And I will set up three shouts at this very gate, than which none were ever more deadly, from the top of Pengwaed in Cornwall to the bottom of Dinsol, in the North, and to Esgair Oervel, in Ireland. And all the women in this Palace that are pregnant shall lose their offspring; and such as are not pregnant, their hearts shall be turned by illness, so that they shall never bear children from this day forward."

"What clamour soever thou mayest make," said Glewlwyd Gavaelvawr, "against the laws of Arthur's Palace shalt thou not enter therein, until I first go and speak with Arthur."

Then Glewlwyd went into the Hall. And Arthur said to him, "Hast thou news from the gate?"

"Half of my life is past, and half of thine. I was heretofore in Kaer Se and Asse, in Sach and Salach, in Lotor and Fotor; and I have been heretofore in India the Great and India the Lesser; and I was in the battle of Dau Ynyr, when the twelve hostages were brought from Llychlyn. And I have also been in Europe, and in Africa, and in the islands of Corsica, and in Caer Brythwch, and Brythach, and Verthach; and I was present when formerly thou didst slay the family of Clis the son of Merin, and when thou didst slay Mil Du the son of Ducum, and when thou didst conquer Greece in the East. And I have been in Caer Oeth and Annoeth, and in Caer Nevenhyr; nine supreme sovereigns, handsome men, saw we there, but never did I behold a man of equal dignity with him who is now at the door of the portal."

Then said Arthur, "If walking thou didst enter in here, return thou running. And every one that beholds the light, and every one that opens and shuts the eye, let them shew him respect, and serve him, some with gold-mounted drinking-horns, others with collops cooked and peppered, until food and drink can be prepared for him. It is unbecoming to keep such a man as thou sayest he is, in the wind and the rain."

Said Kai, "By the hand of my friend, if thou wouldest follow my counsel, thou wouldest not break through the laws of the Court because of him."

"Not so, blessed Kai. It is an honour to us to be resorted to, and the greater our courtesy the greater will be our renown, and our fame, and our glory."

And Glewlwyd came to the gate, and opened the gate before him; and although all dismounted upon the horse-block at the gate, yet did he not dismount, but rode in upon his charger. Then said Kilhwch, "Greeting be unto thee, Sovereign Ruler of this Island; and be this greeting no less unto the lowest than unto the highest, and be it equally unto thy guests, and thy warriors, and thy chieftains--let all partake of it as completely as thyself. And complete be thy favour, and thy fame, and thy glory, throughout all this Island."

"Greeting unto thee also," said Arthur; "sit thou between two of my warriors, and thou shalt have minstrels before thee, and thou shalt enjoy the privileges of a king born to a throne, as long as thou remainest here. And when I dispense my presents to the visitors and strangers in this Court, they shall be in thy hand at my commencing."

Said the youth, "I came not here to consume meat and drink; but if I obtain the boon that I seek, I will requite it thee, and extol thee; and if I have it not, I will bear forth thy dispraise to the four quarters of the world, as far as thy renown has extended."

Then said Arthur, "Since thou wilt not remain here, chieftain, thou shalt receive the boon whatsoever thy tongue may name, as far as the wind dries, and the rain moistens, and the sun revolves, and the sea encircles, and the earth extends; save only my ship; and my mantle; and Caledvwlch, my sword; and Rhongomyant, my lance; and Wynebgwrthucher, my shield; and Carnwenhau, my dagger; and Gwenhwyvar, my wife. By the truth of Heaven, thou shalt have it cheerfully, name what thou wilt."

"I would that thou bless my hair."

"That shall be granted thee."

And Arthur took a golden comb, and scissors, whereof the loops were of silver, and he combed his hair. And Arthur inquired of him who he was. "For my heart warms unto thee, and I know that thou art come of my blood. Tell me, therefore, who thou art."

"I will tell thee, " said the youth, "I am Kilhwch, the son of Kilydd, the son of Prince Kelyddon, by Goleuddydd, my mother, the daughter of Prince Anlawdd."

"That is true," said Arthur; "thou art my cousin. Whatsoever boon thou mayest ask, thou shalt receive, be it what it may that thy tongue shall name."

"Pledge the truth of Heaven and the faith of thy kingdom thereof."

"I pledge it thee, gladly."

"I crave of thee then, that thou obtain for me Olwen, the daughter of Yspaddaden Penkawr; and this boon I likewise seek at the hands of thy warriors. I seek it from Kai, and Bedwyr, and Greidawl Galldonyd, and Gwythyr the son of Greidawl, and Greid the son of Eri, and Kynddelig Kyvarwydd, and Tathal Twyll Goleu, and Maelwys the son of Baeddan, and Crychwr the son of Nes, and Cubert the son of Daere, and Percos the son of Poch, and Lluber Beuthach, and Corvil Bervach, and Gwynn the son of Nudd, and Edeyrn the son of Nudd, and Gadwy the son of Geraint, and Prince Fflewddur Fflam, and Ruawn Pebyr the son of Dorath, and Bradwen the son of Moren Mynawc, and Moren Mynawc himself, and Dalldav the son of Kimin Côv, and the son of Alun Dyved, and the son of Saidi, and the son of Gwryon, and Uchtryd Ardywad Kad, and Kynwas Curvagyl, and Gwrhyr Gwarthegvras, and Isperyr Ewingath, and Gallcoyt Govynynat, and Duach, and Grathach, and Nerthach, the sons of Gwawrddur Kyrvach (these men came forth from the confines of hell), and Kilydd Canhastyr, and Canastyr Kanllaw, and Cors Cant-Ewin, and Esgeir Gulhwch Govynkawn, and Drustwrn Hayarn, and Glewlwyd Gavaelvawr, and Lloch

Llawwynnyawc, and Aunwas Adeiniawc, and Sinnoch the
son of Seithved, and Gwennwynwyn the son of Naw, and
Bedyw the son of Seithved, and Gobrwy the son of Echel
Vorddwyttwll, and Echel Vorddwyttwll himself, and Mael
the son of Roycol, and Dadweir Dallpenn, and Garwyli the
son of Gwythawc Gwyr, and Gwythawc Gwyr himself, and
Gormant the son of Ricca, and Menw the son of
Teirgwaedd, and Digon the son of Alar, and Selyf the son of
Smoit, and Gusg the son of Atheu, and Nerth the son of
Kedarn, and Drudwas the son of Tryffin, and Twrch the son
of Perif, and Twrch the son of Annwas, and Iona king of
France, and Sel the son of Selgi, and Teregud the son of Iaen,
and Sulyen the son of Iaen, and Bradwen the son of Iaen,
and Moren the son of Iaen, and Siawn the son of Iaen, and
Cradawc the son of Iaen. (They were men of Caerdathal, of
Arthur's kindred on his father's side.) Dirmyg the son of
Kaw, and Justic the son of Kaw, and Etmic the son of Kaw,
and Anghawd the son of Kaw, and Ovan the son of Kaw,
and Kelin the son of Kaw, and Connyn the son of Kaw, and
Mabsant the son of Kaw, and Gwyngad the son of Kaw, and
Llwybyr the son of Kaw, and Coth the son of Kaw, and
Meilic the son of Kaw, and Kynwas the son of Kaw, and
Ardwyad the son of Kaw, and Ergyryad the son of Kaw, and
Neb the son of Kaw, and Gilda the son of Kaw, and Calcas
the son of Kaw, and Hueil the son of Kaw (he never yet
made a request at the hand of any Lord). And Samson
Vinsych, and Taliesin the chief of the bards, and
Manawyddan the son of Llyr, and Llary the son of Prince
Kasnar, and Ysperni the son of Fflergant king of Armorica,
and Saranhon, the son of Glythwyr, and Llawr Eilerw, and
Annyanniawc the son of Menw the son of Teirgwaedd, and
Gwynn the son of Nwyvre, and Fflam the son of Nwyvre,
and Geraint the son of Erbin, and Ermid the son of Erbin,
and Dyvel the son of Erbin, and Gwynn the son of Ermid,
and Kyndrwyn the son of Ermid, and Hyveidd Unllenn,
and Eiddon Vawr Vrydic, and Reidwn Arwy, and Gormant

the son of Ricca (Arthur's brother by his mother's side; the Penhynev of Cornwall was his father), and Llawnrodded Varvawc, and Nodawl Varyf Twrch, and Berth the son of Kado, and Rheidwn the son of Beli, and Iscovan Hael, and Iscawin the son of Panon, and Morvran the son of Tegid (no one struck him in the battle of Camlan by reason of his ugliness; all thought he was an auxiliary devil. Hair had he upon him like the hair of a stag). And Sandde Bryd Angel (no one touched him with a spear in the battle of Camlan because of his beauty; all thought he was a ministering angel). And Kynwyl Sant (the third man that escaped from the battle of Camlan, and he was the last who parted from Arthur on Hengroen his horse). And Uchtryd the son of Erim, and Eus the son of Erim, and Henwas Adeinawg the son of Erim, and Henbedestyr the son of Erim, and Sgilti Yscawndroed the son of Erim. (Unto these three men belonged these three qualities,--With Henbedestyr there was not any one who could keep pace, either on horseback or on foot; with Henwas Adeinawg, no four-footed beast could run the distance of an acre, much less could it go beyond it; and as to Sgilti Yscawndroed, when he intended to go upon a message for his Lord, he never sought to find a path, but knowing whither he was to go, if his way lay through a wood he went along the tops of the trees. During his whole life, a blade of reed grass bent not beneath his feet, much less did one ever break, so lightly did he tread.) Teithi Hên the son of Gwynhan (his dominions were swallowed up by the sea, and he himself hardly escaped, and he came to Arthur; and his knife had this peculiarity, that from the time that he came there no haft would ever remain upon it, and owing to this a sickness came over him, and he pined away during the remainder of his life, and of this he died). And Carneddyr the son of Govynyon Hên, and Gwenwynwyn the son of Nav Gyssevin, Arthur's champion, and Llysgadrudd Emys, and Gwrbothu Hên, (uncles unto Arthur were they, his mother's brothers).

Kulvanawyd the son of Goryon, and Llenlleawg Wyddel from the headland of Ganion, and Dyvynwal Moel, and Dunard king of the North, Teirnon Twryf Bliant, and Tegvan Gloff, and Tegyr Talgellawg, Gwrdinal the son of Ebrei, and Morgant Hael, Gwystyl the son of Rhun the son of Nwython, and Llwyddeu the son of Nwython, and Gwydre the son of Llwyddeu (Gwenabwy the daughter of [Kaw] was his mother, Hueil his uncle stabbed him, and hatred was between Hueil and Arthur because of the wound). Drem the son of Dremidyd (when the gnat arose in the morning with the sun, he could see it from Gelli Wic in Cornwall, as far off as Pen Blathaon in North Britain.) And Eidyol the son of Ner, and Glywyddn Saer (who constructed Ehangwen, Arthur's Hall). Kynyr Keinvarvawc (when he was told he had a son born he said to his wife, 'Damsel, if thy son be mine, his heart will be always cold, and there will be no warmth in his hands; and he will have another peculiarity, if he is my son he will always be stubborn; and he will have another peculiarity, when he carries a burden, whether it be large or small, no one will be able to see it, either before him or at his back; and he will have another peculiarity, no one will be able to resist fire and water so well as he will; and he will have another peculiarity, there will never be a servant or an officer equal. to him'). Henwas, and Henwyneb (an old companion to Arthur). Gwallgoyc (another; when he came to a town, though there were three hundred houses in it, if he wanted anything, he would not let sleep come to the eyes of any one whilst he remained there). Berwyn, the son of Gerenhir, and Paris king of France, and Osla Gyllellvawr (who bore a short broad dagger. When Arthur and his hosts came before a torrent, they would seek for a narrow place where they might pass the water, and would lay the sheathed dagger across the torrent, and it would form a bridge sufficient for the armies of the three Islands of Britain, and of the three islands adjacent, with their spoil). Gwyddawg the son of

Menestyr (who slew Kai, and whom Arthur slew, together
with his brothers, to revenge Kai). Garanwyn the son of Kai,
and Amren the son of Bedwyr, and Ely Amyr, and Rheu
Rhwyd Dyrys, and Rhun Rhudwern, and Eli, and
Trachmyr (Arthur's chief huntsmen). And Llwyddeu the
son of Kelcoed, and Hunabwy the son of Gwryon, and
Gwynn Godyvron, and Gweir Datharwenniddawg, and
Gweir the son of Cadell the son of Talaryant, and Gweir
Gwrhyd Ennwir, and Gweir Paladyr Hir (the uncles of
Arthur, the brothers of his mother). The sons of Llwch
Llawwynnyawg (from beyond the raging sea). Llenlleawg
Wyddel, and Ardderchawg Prydain. Cas the son of Saidi,
Gwrvan Gwallt Avwyn, and Gwyllennhin the king of
France, and Gwittart the son of Oedd king of Ireland,
Garselit Wyddel, Panawr Pen Bagad, and Ffleudor the son of
Nav, Gwynnhyvar mayor of Cornwall and Devon (the
ninth man that rallied the battle of Camlan). Keli and
Kueli, and Gilla Coes Hydd (he would clear three hundred
acres at one bound: the chief leaper of Ireland was he). Sol,
and Gwadyn Ossol, and Gawdyn Odyeith. (Sol could stand
all day upon one foot . Gwadyn Ossol, if he stood upon the
top of the highest mountain in the world, it would become
a level plain under his feet. Gwadyn Odyeith, the soles of
his feet emitted sparks of fire when they struck upon things
hard, like the heated mass when drawn out of the forge. He
cleared the way for Arthur when he came to any stoppage.)
Hirerwm and Hiratrwm. (The day they went on a visit
three Cantrevs provided for their entertainment, and they
feasted until noon and drank until night, when they went
to sleep. And then they devoured the heads of the vermin
through hunger, as if they had never eaten anything. When
they made a visit they left neither the fat nor the lean,
neither the hot nor the cold, the sour nor the sweet, the
fresh nor the salt, the boiled nor the raw.) Huarwar the son
of Aflawn (who asked Arthur such a boon as would satisfy
him. It was the third great plague of Cornwall when he

received it. None could get a smile from him but when he was satisfied.) Gware Gwallt Euryn. The two cubs of Gast Rhymi, Gwyddrud and Gwyddneu Astrus. Sugyn the son of Sugnedydd (who would suck up the sea on which were three hundred ships, so as to leave nothing but a dry strand. He was broad-chested). Rhacymwri, the attendant of Arthur (whatever barn he was shown, were there the produce of thirty ploughs within it, he would strike it with an iron flail until the rafters, the beams, and the boards were no better than the small oats in the mow upon the floor of the barn). Dygyflwng, and Anoeth Veidawg. And Hir Eiddyl, and Hir Amreu (they were two attendants of Arthur). And Gwevyl the son of Gwestad (on the day that he was sad, he would let one of his lips drop below his waist, while he turned upon the other like a cap upon his head). Uchtryd Varyf Draws (who spread his red untrimmed beard over the eight-and-forty rafters which were in Arthur's Hall). Elidyr Gyvarwydd. Yskyrdav, the Yscudydd (two attendants of Gwenhywyvar were they. Their feet were swift as their thoughts when bearing a message). Brys the son of Bryssethach (from the Hill of the Black Fernbrake in North Britain). And Grudlwyn Gorr. Bwlch, and Kyfwlch, and Sefwlch, the sons of Cleddyf Kyfwlch, the grandsons of Cleddyf Difwlch. (Their three shields were three gleaming glitterers; their three spears were three pointed piercers; their three swords were three griding gashers; Glas, Glessic, and Gleisad. Their three dogs, Call, Cuall, and Cavall. Their three horses, Hwyrdyddwd, and Drwgdyddwd, and Llwyrdyddwg. Their three wives, Och, and Garym, and Diaspad. Their three grandchildren, Lluched, and Neved, and Eissiwed. Their three daughters, Drwg, and Gwaeth, and Gwaethav Oll. Their three handmaids, Eheubryd the daughter of Kyfwlch, Gorascwrn the daughter of Nerth, Ewaedan the daughter of Kynvelyn Keudawd Pwyll the half-man). Dwnn Diessic Unbenn, Eiladyr the son of Pen Llarcau, Kynedyr Wyllt the son of Hettwn Talaryant, Sawyl

Ben Uchel, Gwalchmai the son of Gwyar, Gwalhaved the
son of Gwyar, Gwrhyr Gwastawd Ieithoedd (to whom all
tongues were known), and Kethcrwm the Priest. Clust the
son of Clustveinad (though he were buried seven cubits
beneath the earth, he would hear the ant fifty miles off rise
from her nest in the morning). Medyr the son of
Methredydd (from Gelli Wic he could, in a twinkling,
shoot the wren through the two legs upon Esgeir Oervel in
Ireland). Gwiawn Llygad Cath (who could cut a haw from
the eye of the gnat without hurting him). Ol the son of
Olwydd (seven years before he was born his father's swine
were carried off, and when he grew up a man he tracked the
swine, and brought them back in seven herds). Bedwini the
Bishop (who blessed Arthur's meat and drink). For the sake
of the golden-chained daughters of this island. For the sake
of Gwenhwyvar its chief lady, and Gwennhwyach her sister,
and Rathtyeu the only daughter of Clemenhill, and
Rhelemon the daughter of Kai, and Tannwen the daughter
of Gweir Datharwenîddawg. Gwenn Alarch the daughter of
Kynwyl Canbwch. Eurneid the daughter of Clydno Eiddin.
Eneuawc the daughter of Bedwyr. Enrydreg the daughter of
Tudvathar. Gwennwledyr the daughter of Gwaledyr
Kyrvach. Erddudnid the daughter of Tryffin. Eurolwen the
daughter of Gwdolwyn Gorr. Teleri the daughter of Peul.
Indeg the daughter of Garwy Hir. Morvudd the daughter
of Urien Rheged. Gwenllian Deg the majestic maiden.
Creiddylad the daughter of Lludd Llaw Ereint. (She was the
most splendid maiden in the three Islands of the mighty,
and in the three Islands adjacent, and for her Gwythyr the
son of Greidawl and Gwynn the son of Nudd fight every
first of May until the day of doom.) Ellylw the daughter of
Neol Kynn-Crog (she lived three ages). Essyllt Vinwen, and
Essyllt Vingul." And all these did Kilhwch son of Kilydd
adjure to obtain his boon.

Then said Arthur, "Oh! Chieftain, I have never heard of
the maiden of whom thou speakest, nor of her kindred, but

I will gladly send messengers in search of her. Give me time to seek her."

And the youth said, "I will willingly grant from this night to that at the end of the year to do so."

Then Arthur sent messengers to every land within his dominions to seek for the maiden; and at the end of the year Arthur's messengers returned without having gained any knowledge or intelligence concerning Olwen more than on the first day.

Then said Kilhwch, "Every one has received his boon, and I yet lack mine. I will depart and bear away thy honour with me."

Then said Kai, "Rash chieftain! doest thou reproach Arthur? Go with us, and we will not part until thou dost either confess that the maiden exists not in the world, or until we obtain her." Thereupon Kai rose up. Kai had this peculiarity, that his breath lasted nine nights and nine days under water, and he could exist nine nights and nine days without sleep. A wound from Kai's sword no physician could heal. Very subtle was Kai. When it pleased him he could render himself as tall as the highest tree in the forest. And he had another peculiarity,--so great was the heat of his nature, that, when it rained hardest, whatever he carried remained dry for a handbreadth above and a handbreadth below his hand; and when his companions were coldest, it was to them as fuel with which to light their fire.

And Arthur called Bedwyr, who never shrank from any enterprise upon which Kai was bound. None was equal to him in swiftness throughout this Island except Arthur and Drych Ail Kibddar. And although he was one-handed, three warriors could not shed blood faster than he on the field of battle. Another property he had; his lance would produce a wound equal to those of nine opposing lances.

And Arthur called to Kynddelig the Guide, "Go thou upon this expedition with the chieftain." For as good a guide was he in a land which he had never seen as he was in his own.

He called Gwrhyr Gwalstawt Ieithoedd, because he knew all tongues.

He called Gwalchmai the son of Gwyar, because he never returned home without achieving the adventure of which he went in quest. He was the best of footmen and the best of knights. He was nephew to Arthur, the son of his sister, and his cousin.

And Arthur called Menw the son of Teirgwaedd, in order that if they went into a savage country, he might cast a charm and an illusion over them, so that none might see them whilst they could see every one.

Part 2

THEY JOURNEYED UNTIL THEY came to a vast open plain, wherein they saw a great castle, which was the fairest of the castles of the world. And they journeyed that day until the evening, and when they thought they were nigh to the castle, they were no nearer to it than they had been in the morning. And the second and the third day they journeyed, and even then scarcely could they reach so far. And when they came before the castle, they beheld a vast flock of sheep, which was boundless and without an end. And upon the top of a mound there was a herdsman, keeping the sheep. And a rug made of skins was upon him; and by his side was a shaggy mastiff, larger than a steed nine winters old. Never had he lost even a lamb from his flock, much less a large sheep. He let no occasion ever pass without doing some hurt and harm. All the dead trees and bushes in the plain he burnt with his breath down to the very ground.

Then said Kai, "Gwrhyr Gwalstawt Ieithoedd, go thou and salute yonder man."

"Kai," said he, "I engaged not to go further than thou thyself."

"Let us go then together," answered Kai.

Said Menw the son of Teirgwaedd, "Fear not to go thither, for I will cast a spell upon the dog, so that he shall injure no one." And they went up to the mound whereon the herdsman was, and they said to him, "How dost thou fare? O herdsman!"

"No less fair be it to you than to me."

"Truly, art thou the chief?" "There is no hurt to injure me but my own."

"Whose are the sheep that thou dost keep, and to whom does yonder castle belong?"

"Stupid are ye, truly! Through the whole world is it known that this is the castle of Yspaddaden Penkawr."

"And who art thou?"

"I am called Custennin the son of Dyfnedig, and my brother Yspaddaden Penkawr oppressed me because of my possessions. And ye also, who are ye?"

"We are an embassy from Arthur, come to seek Olwen the daughter of Yspaddaden Penkawr."

"Oh men! the mercy of Heaven be upon you, do not that for all the world. None who ever came hither on this quest has returned alive." And the herdsman rose up. And as he arose, Kilhwch gave unto him a ring of gold. And he sought to put on the ring, but it was too small for him, so he placed it in the finger of his glove. And he went home, and gave the glove to his spouse to keep. And she took the ring from the glove when it was given her, and she said, "Whence came this ring, for thou art not wont to have good fortune?"

"I went," said he, "to the sea to seek for fish, and lo, I saw a corpse borne by the waves. And a fairer corpse than it did I never behold. And from its finger did I take this ring."

"O man! does the sea permit its dead to wear jewels? Show me then this body."

"O wife, him to whom this ring belonged thou shalt see here in the evening."

"And who is he?" asked the woman. "Kilhwch the son of Kilydd, the son of Prince Kelyddon, by Goleuddydd the daughter of Prince Anlawdd, his mother, who is come to seek Olwen as his wife." And when she heard that, her feelings were divided between the joy that she had that her nephew, the son of her sister, was coming to her, and sorrow because she had never known any one depart alive who had come on that quest.

And they went forward to the gate of Custennin the herdsman's dwelling. And when she heard their footsteps approaching, she ran out with joy to meet them. And Kai snatched a billet out of the pile. And when she met them she sought to throw her arms about their necks. And Kai placed the log between her two hands, and she squeezed it so that it became a twisted coil. "Oh woman," said Kai, "if thou hadst squeezed me thus, none could ever again have set their affections on me. Evil love were this." They entered into the house, and were served; and soon after they all went forth to amuse themselves. Then the woman opened a stone chest that was before the chimney-corner, and out of it arose a youth with yellow curling hair. Said Gwrhyr, "It is a pity to hide this youth. I know that it is not his own crime that is thus visited upon him."

"This is but a remnant," said the woman. "Three-and-twenty of my sons has Yspaddaden Penkawr slain, and I have no more hope of this one than of the others."

Then said Kai, "Let him come and be a companion with me, and he shall not be slain unless I also am slain with him." And they ate.

And the woman asked them, "Upon what errand come you here?"

"We come to seek Olwen for this youth."

Then said the woman, "In the name of Heaven, since no one from the castle hath yet seen you, return again whence you came."

"Heaven is our witness, that we will not return until we have seen the maiden."

Said Kai, "Does she ever come hither, so that she may be seen?"

"She comes here every Saturday to wash her head, and in the vessel where she washes, she leaves all her rings, and she never either comes herself or sends any messengers to fetch them."

"Will she come here if she is sent to?"

"Heaven knows that I will not destroy my soul, nor will I betray those that trust me; unless you will pledge me your faith that you will not harm her, I will not send to her."

"We pledge it," said they. So a message was sent, and she came.

The maiden was clothed in a robe of flame-coloured silk, and about her neck was a collar of ruddy gold, on which were precious emeralds and rubies. More yellow was her head than the flower of the broom, and her skin was whiter than the foam of the wave, and fairer were her hands and her fingers than the blossoms of the wood anemone amidst the spray of the meadow fountain. The eye of the trained hawk, the glance of the three-mewed falcon was not brighter than hers. Her bosom was more snowy than the breast of the white swan, her cheek was redder than the reddest roses. Whoso beheld her was filled with her love. Four white trefoils sprung up wherever she trod. And therefore was she called Olwen.

She entered the house, and sat beside Kilhwch upon the foremost bench; and as soon as he saw her he knew her. And Kilhwch said unto her, "Ah! maiden, thou art she whom I have loved; come away with me, lest they speak evil of thee and of me. Many a day have I loved thee."

"I cannot do this, for I have pledged my faith to my father not to go without his counsel, for his life will last only until the time of my espousals. Whatever is, must be. But I will give thee advice if thou wilt take it. Go, ask me of my father, and that which he shall require of thee, grant it, and thou wilt obtain me; but it thou deny him anything, thou wilt not obtain me, and it will be well for thee if thou escape with thy life."

"I promise all this, if occasion offer," said he.

She returned to her chamber, and they all rose up and followed her to the castle. And they slew the nine porters that were at the nine gates in silence. And they slew the nine watch-dogs without one of them barking. And they went forward to the hall.

"The greeting of heaven and of man be unto thee, Yspaddaden Penkawr," said they. "And you, wherefore come you?"

"We come to ask thy daughter Olwen, for Kilhwch the son of Kilydd, the son of Prince Kelyddon."

"Where are my pages and my servants? Raise up the forks beneath my two eyebrows which have fallen over my eyes, that I may see the fashion of my son-in-law." And they did so. "Come hither to-morrow, and you shall have an answer."

They rose to go forth, and Yspaddaden Penkawr seized one of the three poisoned darts that lay beside him, and threw it after them. And Bedwyr caught it, and flung it, and pierced Yspaddaden Penkawr grievously with it through the knee. Then he said, "A cursed ungentle son-in-law, truly. I shall ever walk the worse for his rudeness, and shall ever be without a cure. This poisoned iron pains me like the bite of a gadfly. Cursed be the smith who forged it, and the anvil whereon it was wrought! So sharp is it!"

That night also they took up their abode in the house of Custennin the herdsman. The next day with the dawn, they arrayed themselves in haste and proceeded to the castle, and entered the hall, and they said, "Yspaddaden Penkawr, give us thy daughter in consideration of her dower and her maiden fee, which we will pay to thee and to her two kinswomen likewise. And unless thou wilt do so, thou shalt meet with thy death on her account." Then he said, "Her four great-grandmothers, and her four great-grandsires are yet alive, it is needful that I take counsel of them."

"Be it so," answered they, "we will go to meat." As they rose up, he took the second dart that was beside him, and cast it after them. And Menw the son of Gwaedd caught it, and flung it back at him, and wounded him in the centre of the breast, so that it came out at the small of his back. "A cursed ungentle son-in-law, truly," said he, "the hard iron pains me like the bite of a horse-leech. Cursed be the hearth whereon it was heated, and the smith who formed it! So sharp is it! Henceforth, whenever I go up a hill, I shall have a scant in my breath, and a pain in my chest, and I shall often loathe my food." And they went to meat.

And the third day they returned to the palace. And Yspaddaden Penkawr said to them, "Shoot not at me again unless you desire death. Where are my attendants? Lift up the forks of my eyebrows which have fallen over my eyeballs, that I may see the fashion of my son-in-law." Then they arose, and, as they did so, Yspaddaden Penkawr took the third poisoned dart and cast it at them. And Kilhwch caught it and threw it vigorously, and wounded him through the eyeball, so that the dart came out at the back of his head. "A cursed ungentle son-in-law, truly! As long as I remain alive, my eyesight will be the worse. Whenever I go against the wind, my eyes will water; and peradventure my head will burn, and I shall have a giddiness every new moon. Cursed be the fire in which it was forged. Like the bite of a mad dog is the stroke of this poisoned iron." And they went to meat.

And the next day they came again to the palace, and they said, "Shoot not at us any more, unless thou desirest such hurt, and harm, and torture as thou now hast, and even more."

"Give me thy daughter, and if thou wilt not give her, thou shalt receive thy death because of her."

"Where is he that seeks my daughter? Come hither where I may see thee." And they placed him a chair face to face with him.

Said Yspaddaden Penkawr, "Is it thou that seekest my daughter?"

"It is I," answered Kilhwch.

"I must have thy pledge that thou wilt not do towards me otherwise than is just, and when I have gotten that which I shall name, my daughter thou shalt have."

"I promise thee that willingly," said Kilhwch, "name what thou wilt."

"I will do so," said he.

"Seest thou yonder vast hill?" "I see it." "I require that it be rooted up, and that the grubbings be burned for manure on the face of the land, and that it be ploughed and sown in one day, and in one day that the grain ripen. And of that wheat I intend to make food and liquor fit for the wedding of thee and my daughter. And all this I require done in one day."

"It will be easy for me to compass this, although thou mayest think that it will not be easy."

"Though this be easy for thee, there is yet that which will not be so. No husbandman can till or prepare this land, so wild is it, except Amaethon the son of Don, and he will not come with thee by his own free will, and thou wilt not be able to compel him.

"It will be easy for me to compass this, although thou mayest think that it will not be easy."

"Though thou get this, there is yet that which thou wilt not get. Govannon the son of Don to come to the headland to rid the iron, he will do no work of his own good will except for a lawful king, and thou wilt not be able to compel him."

"It will be easy for me to compass this."

"Though thou get this, there is yet that which thou wilt not get; the two dun oxen of Gwlwlyd, both yoked together, to plough the wild land yonder stoutly. He will not give them of his own free will, and thou wilt not be able to compel him."

"It will be easy for me to compass this."

"Though thou get this, there is yet that which thou wilt not get; the yellow and the brindled bull yoked together do I require."

"It will be easy for me to compass this."

"Though thou get this, there is yet that which thou wilt not get; the two horned oxen, one of which is beyond, and the other this side of the peaked mountain, yoked together in the same plough. And these are Nynniaw and Peibaw, whom God turned into oxen on account of their sins."

"It will be easy for me to compass this."

"Though thou get this, there is yet that which thou wilt not get. Seest thou yonder red tilled ground?"

"I see it."

"When first I met the mother of this maiden, nine bushels of flax were sown therein, and none has yet sprung up, neither white nor black; and I have the measure by me still. I require to have the flax to sow in the new land under, that when it grows up it may make a white wimple, for my daughter's head, on the day of thy wedding."

"It will be easy for me to compass this, although thou mayest think that it will not be easy."

"Though thou gets this, there is yet that which thou wilt not get. Honey that is nine times sweeter than the honey of the virgin swarm, without scum and bees, do I require to make bragget for the feast."

"It will be easy for me to compass this, although thou mayest think that it will not be easy."

"The vessel of Llwyr the son of Llwyryon, which is of the utmost value. There is no other vessel in the world that can hold this drink. Of his free will thou wilt not get it, and thou canst not compel him."

"It will be easy for me to compass this, although thou mayest think that it will not be easy."

"Though thou get this, there is yet that which thou wilt not get. The basket of Gwyddneu Garanhir, if the whole world should come together, thrice nine men at a time, the meat that each of them desired would be found within it. I require to eat therefrom on the night that my daughter becomes thy bride. He will give it to no one of his own free will, and thou canst not compel him."

"It will be easy for me to compass this, although thou mayest think that it will not be easy."

"Though thou get this, there is yet that which thou wilt not get. The horn of Gwlgawd Gododin to serve us with liquor that night. He will not give it of his own free will, and thou wilt not be able to compel him."

"It will be easy for me to compass this, although thou mayest think that it will not be easy."

"Though thou get this, there is yet that which thou wilt not get. The harp of Teirtu to play to us that night. When a man desires that it should play, it does so of itself, and when he desires that it should cease, it ceases. And this he will not give of his own free will, and thou wilt not be able to compel him."

"It will be easy for me to compass this, although thou mayest think that it will not be easy."

"Though thou get this, there is yet that which thou wilt not get. The cauldron of Diwrnach Wyddel, the steward of Odgar the son of Aedd, king of Ireland, to boil the meat for thy marriage feast."

"It will be easy for me to compass this, although thou mayest think that it will not be easy."

"Though thou get this, there is yet that which thou wilt not get. It is needful for me to wash my head, and shave my beard, and I require the tusk of Yskithyrwyn Benbaedd to shave myself withal, neither shall I profit by its use if it be not plucked alive out of his head."

"It will be easy for me to compass this, although thou mayest think that it will not be easy."

"Though thou get this, there is yet that which thou wilt not get. There is no one in the world that can pluck it out of his head except Odgar the son of Aedd, king of Ireland."

"It will be easy for me to compass this."

"Though thou get this, there is yet that which thou wilt not get. I will not trust any one to keep the tusk except Gado of North Britain. Now the threescore Cantrevs of North Britain are under his sway, and of his own free will he will not come out of his kingdom, and thou wilt not be able to compel him."

"It will be easy for me to compass this, although thou mayest think that it will not be easy."

"Though thou get this, there is yet that which thou wilt not get. I must spread out my hair in order to shave it, and it will never be spread out unless I have the blood of the jet black sorceress, the daughter of the pure white sorceress, from Pen Nant Govid, on the confines of Hell."

"It will be easy for me to compass this, although thou mayest think that it will not be easy."

"Though thou get this, there is yet that which thou wilt not get. I will not have the blood unless I have it warm, and no vessels will keep warm the liquid that is put therein except the bottles of Gwyddolwyn Gorr, which preserve the heat of the liquor that is put into them in the east, until they arrive at the west. And he will not give them of his own free will, and thou wilt not be able to compel him."

"It will be easy for me to compass this, although thou mayest think that it will not be easy."

"Though thou get this, there is yet that which thou wilt not get. Some will desire fresh milk, and it will not be possible to have fresh milk for all, unless we have the bottles of Rhinnon Rhin Barnawd, wherein no liquor ever turns sour. And he will not give them of his own free will, and thou wilt not be able to compel him."

"It will be easy for me to compass this, although thou mayest think that it will not be easy."

"Though thou get this, there is yet that which thou wilt not get. Throughout the world there is not a comb or scissors with which I can arrange my hair, on account of its rankness, except the comb and scissors that are between the two ears of Twrch Trwyth, the son of Prince Tared. He will not give them of his own free will, and thou wilt not be able to compel him."

"It will be easy for me to compass this, although thou mayest think that it will not be easy."

"Though thou get this, there is yet that which thou wilt not get. It will not be possible to hunt Twrch Trwyth without Drudwyn the whelp of Greid, the son of Eri."

"It will be easy for me to compass this, although thou mayest think that it will not be easy."

"Though thou get this, there is yet that which thou wilt not get. Throughout the world there is not a leash that can hold him, except the leash of Cwrs Cant Ewin."

"It will be easy for me to compass this, although thou mayest think that it will not be easy."

"Though thou get this, there is yet that which thou wilt not get. Throughout the world there is no collar that will hold the leash except the collar of Canhastyr Canllaw."

"It will be easy for me to compass this, although thou mayest think that it will not be easy."

"Though thou get this, there is yet that which thou wilt not get. The chain of Kilydd Canhastyr to fasten the collar to the leash."

"It will be easy for me to compass this, although thou mayest think that it will not be easy."

"Though thou get this, there is yet that which thou wilt not get. Throughout the world there is not a huntsman who can hunt with this dog, except Mabon the son of Modron. He was taken from his mother when three nights old, and it is not known where he now is, nor whether he is living or dead."

"It will be easy for me to compass this, although thou mayest think that it will not be easy."

"Though thou get this, there is yet that which thou wilt not get. Gwynn Mygdwn, the horse of Gweddw, that is as swift as the wave, to carry Mabon the son of Modron to hunt the boar Trwyth. He will not give him of his own free will, and thou wilt not be able to compel him."

"It will be easy for me to compass this, although thou mayest think that it will not be easy."

"Though thou get this, there is yet that which thou wilt not get. Thou wilt not get Mabon, for it is not known where he is, unless thou find Eidoel, his kinsman in blood, the son of Aer. For it would be useless to seek for him. He is his cousin."

"It will be easy for me to compass this, although thou mayest think that it will not be easy."

"Though thou get this, there is yet that which thou wilt not get. Garselit the Gwyddelian is the chief huntsman of Ireland; the Twrch Trwyth can never be hunted without him."

"It will be easy for me to compass this, although thou mayest think that it will not be easy."

"Though thou get this, there is yet that which thou wilt not get. A leash made from the beard of Dissull Varvawc, for that is the only one that can hold those two cubs. And the leash will be of no avail unless it be plucked from his beard while he is alive, and twitched out with wooden tweezers. While he lives he will not suffer this to be done to him, and the leash will be of no use should he be dead, because it will be brittle."

"It will be easy for me to compass this, although thou mayest think that it will not be easy."

"Though thou get this, there is yet that which thou wilt not get. Throughout the world there is no huntsman that can hold those two whelps except Kynedyr Wyllt, the son of Hettwn Glafyrawc; he is nine times more wild than the wildest beast upon the mountains. Him wilt thou never get, neither wilt thou ever get my daughter."

"It will be easy for me to compass this, although thou mayest think that it will not be easy."

"Though thou get this, there is yet that which thou wilt not get. It is not possible to hunt the boar Trwyth without Gwynn the son of Nudd, whom God has placed over the brood of devils in Annwn, lest they should destroy the present race. He will never be spared thence."

"It will be easy for me to compass this, although thou mayest think that it will not be easy."

"Though thou get this, there is yet that which thou wilt not get. There is not a horse in the world that can carry Gwynn to hunt the Twrch Trwyth, except Du, the horse of Mor of Oerveddawg."

"It will be easy for me to compass this, although thou mayest think that it will not be easy."

"Though thou get this, there is yet that which thou wilt not get. Until Gilennhin the king of France shall come, the Twrch Trwyth cannot be hunted. It will be unseemly for him to leave his kingdom for thy sake, and he will never come hither."

"It will be easy for me to compass this, although thou mayest think that it will not be easy."

"Though thou get this, there is yet that which thou wilt not get. The Twrch Trwyth can never be hunted without the son of Alun Dyved; he is well skilled in letting loose the dogs."

"It will be easy for me to compass this, although thou mayest think that it will not be easy."

"Though thou get this, there is yet that which thou wilt not get. The Twrch Trwyth cannot be hunted unless thou get Aned and Aethlem. They are as swift as the gale of wind, and they were never let loose upon a beast that they did not kill him."

"It will be easy for me to compass this, although thou mayest think that it will not be easy."

"Though thou get this, there is yet that which thou wilt not get; Arthur and his companions to hunt the Twrch Trwyth. He is a mighty man, and he will not come for thee, neither wilt thou be able to compel him."

"It will be easy for me to compass this, although thou mayest think that it will not be easy."

"Though thou get this there is yet that which thou wilt not get. The Twrch Trwyth cannot be hunted unless thou get Bwlch, and Kyfwlch [and Sefwlch], the grandsons of Cleddyf Difwlch. Their three shields are three gleaming glitterers Their three spears are three pointed piercers. Their three swords are three griding gashers, Glas, Glessic, and Clersag. Their three dogs, Call, Cuall, and Cavall. Their three horses, Hwyrdydwg, and Drwgdydwg, and Llwyrdydwg. Their three wives, Och, and Garam, and Diaspad. Their three grandchildren, Lluched, and Vyned, and Eissiwed. Their three daughters, Drwg, and Gwaeth, and Gwaethav Oll. Their three handmaids [Eheubryd, the daughter of Kyfwlch; Gorasgwrn, the daughter of Nerth; and Gwaedan, the daughter of Kynvelyn]. These three men shall sound the horn, and all the others shall shout, so that all will think that the sky is falling to the earth."

"It will be easy for me to compass this, although thou mayest think that it will not be easy."

"Though thou get this, there is yet that which thou wilt not get. The sword of Gwrnach the Giant; he will never be slain except therewith. O his own free will he will not give it, either for a price or as a gift, and thou wilt never be able to compel him."

"It will be easy for me to compass this, although thou mayest think that it will not be easy."

"Though thou get this, there is yet that which thou wilt not get. Difficulties shalt thou meet with, and nights without sleep, in seeking this, and if thou obtain it not, neither shalt thou obtain my daughter."

"Horses shall I have, and chivalry; and my lord and kinsman Arthur will obtain for me all these things. And I shall gain thy daughter, and thou shalt lose thy life."

"Go forward. And thou shalt not be chargeable for food or raiment for my daughter while thou art seeking these things; and when thou hast compassed all these marvels, thou shalt have my daughter for thy wife."

Part 3

ALL THAT DAY THEY journeyed until the evening, and then they beheld a vast castle, which was the largest in the world. And lo, a black man, huger than three of the men of this world, came out from the castle. And they spoke unto him, "Whence comest thou, O man?"

"From the castle which you see yonder."

"Whose castle is that?" asked they.

"Stupid are ye truly, O men. There is no one in the world that does not know to whom this castle belongs. It is the castle of Gwrnach the Giant."

"What treatment is there for guests and strangers that alight in that castle?"

"Oh! Chieftain, Heaven protect thee. No guest ever returned thence alive, and no one may enter therein unless he brings with him his craft."

Then they proceeded towards the gate. Said Gwrhyr Gwalstawd Ieithoedd, "Is there a porter?"

"There is. And thou, if thy tongue be not mute in thy head, wherefore dost thou call?"

"Open the gate."

"I will not open it."

"Wherefore wilt thou not?"

"The knife is in the meat, and the drink is in the horn, and there is revelry in the hall of Gwrnach the Giant, and except for a craftsman who brings his craft, the gate will not be opened to-night."

"Verily, porter," then said Kai, "my craft bring I with me."

"What is thy craft?"

"The best burnisher of swords am I in the world."

"I will go and tell this unto Gwrnach the Giant, and I will bring thee an answer."

So the porter went in, and Gwrnach said to him, "Hast thou any news from the gate?"

"I have. There is a party at the door of the gate who desire to come in." "Didst thou inquire of them if they possessed any art?"

"I did inquire," said he, "and one told me that he was well skilled in the burnishing of swords."

"We have need of him then. For some time have I sought for some one to polish my sword, and could find no one. Let this man enter, since he brings with him his craft." The porter thereupon returned and opened the gate. And Kai went in by himself, and he saluted Gwrnach the Giant. And a chair was placed for him opposite to Gwrnach. And Gwrnach said to him, "Oh man! is it true that is reported of thee that thou knowest how to burnish swords?"

"I know full well how to do so," answered Kai. Then was the sword of Gwrnach brought to him. And Kai took a blue whetstone from under his arm, and asked him whether he would have it burnished white or blue. "Do with it as it seems good to thee, and as though wouldest if it were thine own." Then Kai polished one half of the blade and put it in his hand. "Will this please thee?" asked he. "I would rather than all that is in my dominions that the whole of it were like unto this. It is a marvel to me that such a man as thou should be without a companion."

"Oh! noble sir, I have a companion, albeit he is not skilled in this art."

"Who may he be?"

"Let the porter go forth and I will tell him whereby he may know him. The head of his lance will leave its shaft, and draw blood from the wind, and will descend upon its shaft again." Then the gate was opened, and Bedwyr entered. And Kai said, "Bedwyr is very skilful, although he knows not this art."

And there was much discourse among those who were without, because that Kai and Bedwyr had gone in. And a young man who was with them, the only son of Custennin the herdsman, got in also. And he caused all his companions to keep close to him as he passed the three wards, and until he came into the midst of the castle. And his companions said unto the son of Custennin, "Thou hast done this! Thou art the best of all men." And thenceforth he was called Goreu, the son of Custennin. Then they dispersed to their lodgings, that they might slay those who lodged therein, unknown to the Giant.

The sword was now polished, and Kai gave it unto the hand of Gwrnach the Giant, to see if he were pleased with his work. And the Giant said, "The work is good, I am content therewith."

Said Kai, "It is thy scabbard that hath rusted thy sword, give it to me that I may take out the wooden sides of it and put in new ones." And he took the scabbard from him, and the sword in the other hand. And he came and stood over against the Giant, as if he would have put the sword into the scabbard; and with it he struck at the head of the Giant, and cut off his head at one blow. Then they despoiled the castle, and took from it what goods and jewels they would. And again on the same day, at the beginning of the year, they came to Arthur's Court, bearing with them the sword of Gwrnach the Giant.

Now, when they told Arthur how they had sped, Arthur said, "Which of these marvels will it be best for us to seek first?"

"It will be best," said they, "to seek Mabon the son of Modron; and he will not be found unless we first find Eidoel, the son of Aer, his kinsman." Then Arthur rose up, and the warriors of the Islands of Britain with him, to seek for Eidoel; and they proceeded until they came before the Castle of Glivi, where Eidoel was imprisoned. Glivi stood on the summit of his castle, and he said, "Arthur, what requirest thou of me, since nothing remains to me in this fortress, and I have neither joy nor pleasure in it; neither wheat nor oats? Seek not therefore to do me harm."

Said Arthur, "Not to injure thee came I hither, but to seek for the prisoner that is with thee."

"I will give thee my prisoner, though I had not thought to give him up to any one; and therewith shalt thou have my support and my aid."

His followers said unto Arthur, "Lord, go thou home, thou canst not proceed with thy host in quest of such small adventures as these."

Then said Arthur, "It were well for thee, Gwrhyr Gwalstawd Ieithoedd, to go upon this quest, for thou knowest all languages, and art familiar with those of the birds and the beasts. Thou, Eidoel, oughtest likewise to go with my men in search of thy cousin. And as for you, Kai and Bedwyr, I have hope of whatever adventure ye are in quest of, that ye will achieve it. Achieve ye this adventure for me."

They went forward until they came to the Ousel of Cilgwri. And Gwrhyr adjured her for the sake of Heaven, saying, "Tell me if thou knowest aught of Mabon the son of Modron, who was taken when three nights old from between his mother and the wall."

And the Ousel answered, "When I first came here, there was a smith's anvil in this place, and I was then a young bird; and from that time no work has been done upon it, save the pecking of my beak every evening, and now there is not so much as the size of a nut remaining thereof; yet the vengeance of Heaven be upon me, if during all that time I have ever heard of the man for whom you inquire. Nevertheless I will do that which is right, and that which it is fitting that I should do for an embassy from Arthur. There is a race of animals who were formed before me, and I will be your guide to them."

So they proceeded to the place where was the Stag of Redynvre. "Stag of Redynvre, behold we are come to thee, an embassy from Arthur, for we have not heard of any animal older than thou. Say, knowest thou aught of Mabon the son of Modron, who was taken from his mother when three nights old?"

The Stag said, "When I first came hither, there was a plain all around me, without any trees save one oak sapling, which grew up to be an oak with an hundred branches. And that oak has since perished, so that now nothing remains of it but the withered stump; and from that day to this I have been here, yet have I never heard of the man for whom you inquire. Nevertheless, being an embassy from Arthur, I will be your guide to the place where there is an animal which was formed before I was."

So they proceeded to the place where was the Owl of Cwm Cawlwyd. "Owl of Cwm Cawlwyd, here is an embassy from Arthur; knowest thou aught of Mabon the son of Modron, who was taken after three nights from his mother?"

"If I knew I would tell you. When first I came hither, the wide valley you see was a wooded glen. And a race of men came and rooted it up. And there grew there a second wood; and this wood is the third. My wings, are they not withered stumps? Yet all this time, even until to-day, I have never heard of the man for whom you inquire. Nevertheless, I will be the guide of Arthur's embassy until you come to the place where is the oldest animal in this world, and the one that has travelled most, the Eagle of Gwern Abwy."

Gwrhyr said, "Eagle of Gwern Abwy, we have come to thee an embassy from Arthur, to ask thee if thou knowest aught of Mabon the son of Modron, who was taken from his mother when he was three nights old." The Eagle said, "I have been here for a great space of time, and when I first came hither there was a rock here, from the top of which I pecked at the stars every evening; and now it is not so much as a span high. From that day to this I have been here, and I have never heard of the man for whom you inquire, except once when I went in search of food as far as Llyn Llyw. And when I came there, I struck my talons into a salmon, thinking he would serve me as food for a long time. But he drew me into the deep, and I was scarcely able to escape from him. After that I went with my whole kindred to attack him, and to try to destroy him, but he sent messengers, and made peace with me; and came and besought me to take fifty fish spears out of his back. Unless he know something of him whom you seek, I cannot tell who may. However, I will guide you to the place where he is.

So they went thither; and the Eagle said, "Salmon of Llyn Llyw, I have come to thee with an embassy from Arthur, to ask thee if thou knowest aught concerning Mabon the son of Modron, who was taken away at three nights old from his mother."

"As much as I know I will tell thee. With every tide I go along the river upwards, until I come near to the walls of Gloucester, and there have I found such wrong as I never found elsewhere; and to the end that ye may give credence thereto, let one of you go thither upon each of my two shoulders." So Kai and Gwrhyr Gwalstawd Ieithoedd went upon the two shoulders of the salmon, and they proceeded until they came unto the wall of the prison, and they heard a great wailing and lamenting from the dungeon. Said Gwrhyr, "Who is it that laments in this house of stone?"

"Alas, there is reason enough for whoever is here to lament. It is Mabon the son of Modron who is here imprisoned; and no imprisonment was ever so grievous as mine, neither that of Lludd Llaw Ereint, nor that of Greid the son of Eri."

"Hast thou hope of being released for gold or for silver, or for any gifts of wealth, or through battle and fighting?"

"By fighting will whatever I may gain be obtained."

Then they went thence, and returned to Arthur, and they told him where Mabon the son of Modron was imprisoned. And Arthur summoned the warriors of the Island, and they journeyed as far as Gloucester, to the place where Mabon was in prison. Kai and Bedwyr went upon the shoulders of the fish, whilst the warriors of Arthur attacked the castle. And Kai broke through the wall into the dungeon, and brought away the prisoner upon his back, whilst the fight was going on between the warriors. And Arthur returned home, and Mabon with him at liberty.

Said Arthur, "Which of the marvels will it be best for us now to seek first?" "It will be best to seek for the two cubs of Gast Rhymhi."

"Is it known," asked Arthur, "where she is!"

"She is in Aber Deu Gleddyf," said one. Then Arthur went to the house of Tringad, in Aber Cleddyf, and he inquired of him whether he had heard of her there. "In what form may she be?"

"She is in the form of a she-wolf," said he; "and with her there are two cubs."

"She has often slain my herds, and she is there below in a cave in Aber Cleddyf."

So Arthur went in his ship Prydwen by sea, and the others went by land, to hunt her. And they surrounded her and her two cubs, and God did change them again for Arthur into their own form. And the host of Arthur dispersed themselves into parties of one and two.

On a certain day, as Gwythyr the son of Greidawl was walking over a mountain, he heard a wailing and a grievous cry. And when he heard it, he sprang forward, and went towards it. And when he came there, he drew his sword, and smote off an ant-hill close to the earth, whereby it escaped being burned in the fire. And the ants said to him, "Receive from us the blessing of heaven, and that which no man can give we will give thee." Then they fetched the nine bushels of flax-seed which Yspaddaden Penkawr had required of Kilhwch, and they brought the full measure without lacking any, except one flax-seed, and that the lame pismire brought in before night.

As Kai and Bedwyr sat on a beacon carn on the summit of Plinlimmon, in the highest wind that ever was in the world, they looked around them, and saw a great smoke towards the south, afar off, which did not bend with the wind. Then said Kai, "By the hand of my friend, behold, yonder is the fire of a robber!" Then they hastened towards the smoke, and they came so near to it, that they could see Dillus Varvawc scorching a wild boar. "Behold, yonder is the greatest robber that ever fled from Arthur," said Bedwyr unto Kai. "Dost thou know him?"

"I do know him," answered Kai, "he is Dillus Varvawc, and no leash in the world will be able to hold Drudwyn, the cub of Greid the son of Eri, save a leash made from the beard of him thou seest yonder. And even that will be useless, unless his beard be plucked alive with wooden tweezers; for if dead, it will be brittle."

"What thinkest thou that we should do concerning this?" said Bedwyr.

"Let us suffer him," said Kai, "to eat as much as he will of the meat, and after that he will fall asleep." And during that time they employed themselves in making the wooden tweezers. And when Kai knew certainly that he was asleep, he made a pit under his feet, the largest in the world, and he struck him a violent plow, and squeezed him into the pit. And there they twitched out his beard completely with the wooden tweezers; and after that they slew him altogether.

And from thence they both went to Gelli Wic, in Cornwall, and took the leash made of Dillus Varvawc's beard with them, and they gave it into Arthur's hand. Then Arthur composed this Englyn--

Kai made a leash

Of Dillus son of Eurei's beard.

Were he alive, thy death he'd be.

And thereupon Kai was wroth, so that the warriors of the Island could scarcely make peace between Kai and Arthur. And thenceforth, neither in Arthur's troubles, nor for the slaying of his men, would Kai come forward to his aid for ever after.

Said Arthur, "Which of the marvels is it best for us now to seek?"

"It is best for us to seek Drudwyn, the cub of Greid the son of Eri."

A little while before this, Creiddylad the daughter of Llud Llaw Ereint, and Gwythyr the son of Greidawl, were betrothed. And before she had become his bride, Gwn ap Nudd came and carried her away by force; and Gwythyr the son of Greidawl gathered his host together, and went to fight with Gwyn ap Nudd. But Gwyn overcame him, and captured Greid the son of Eri, and Glinneu the son of Taran, and Gwrgwst Ledlwm, and Dynvarth his son. And he captured Penn the son of Nethawg, and Nwython, and Kyledyr Wyllt his son. And they slew Nwython, and took out his heart, and constrained Kyledyr to eat the heart of his father. And therefrom Kyledyr became mad. When Arthur heard of this, he went to the North, and summoned Gwyn ap Nudd before him, and set free the nobles whom he had put in prison, and made peace between Gwyn ap Nudd and Gwythyr the son of Greidawl. And this was the peace that was made:--that the maiden should remain in her father's house, without advantage to either of them, and that Gwyn ap Nudd and Gwythyr the son of Greidawl should fight for her every first of May, from thenceforth until the day of doom, and that whichever of them should then be conqueror should have the maiden.

And when Arthur had thus reconciled these chieftains, he obtained Mygdwn, Gweddw's horse, and the leash of Cwrs Cant Ewin.

And after that Arthur went into Armorica, and with him Mabon the son of Mellt, and Gware Gwallt Euryn, to seek the two dogs of Glythmyr Ledewic. And when he had got them, he went to the West of Ireland, in search of Gwrgi Severi; and Odgar the son of Aedd king of Ireland, went with him. And thence went Arthur into the North, and captured Kyledyr Wyllt; and he went after Yskithyrwyn Benbaedd. And Mabon the son of Mellt came with the two dogs of Glythmyr Ledewic in his hand, and Drudwyn, the cub of Greid the son of Eri. And Arthur went himself to the chase, leading his own dog Cavall. And Kaw, of North Britain, mounted Arthur's mare Llamrei, and was first in the attack. Then Kaw, of North Britain, wielded a mighty axe, and absolutely daring he came valiantly up to the boar, and clave his head in twain. And Kaw took away the tusk. Now the boar was not slain by the dogs that Yspaddaden had mentioned, but by Cavall, Arthur's own dog.

And after Yskithyrwyn Penbaedd was killed, Arthur and his host departed to Gelli Wic in Cornwall. And thence he sent Menw the son of Teirgwaedd to see if the precious things were between the two ears of Twrch Trwyth, since it were useless to encounter him if they were not there. Albeit it was certain where he was, for he had laid waste the third part of Ireland. And Menw went to seek for him, and he met with him in Ireland, in Esgeir Oervel. And Menw took the form of a bird; and he descended upon the top of his lair, and strove to snatch away one of the precious things from him, but he carried away nothing but one of his bristles. And the boar rose up angrily and shook himself so that some of his venom fell upon Menw, and he was never well from that day forward.

After this Arthur sent an embassy to Odgar, the son of Aedd king of Ireland, to ask for the Cauldron of Diwrnach Wyddel, his purveyor. And Odgar commanded him to give it. But Diwrnach said, "Heaven is my witness, if it would avail him anything even to look at it, he should not do so." And the embassy of Arthur returned from Ireland with this denial. And Arthur set forward with a small retinue, and entered into Prydwen, his ship, and went over to Ireland. And they proceeded into the house of Diwrnach Wyddel. And the hosts of Odgar saw their strength. When they had eaten and drunk as much as they desired, Arthur demanded to have the cauldron. And he answered, "If I would have given it to any one, I would have given it at the word of Odgar king of Ireland."

When he had given them this denial, Bedwyr arose and seized hold of the cauldron, and placed it upon the back of Hygwyd, Arthur's servant, who was brother, by the mother's side, to Arthur's servant, Cachamwri. His office was always to carry Arthur's cauldron, and to place fire under it. And Llenlleawg Wyddel seized Caledvwlch, and brandished it. And they slew Diwrnach Wyddel and his company. Then came the Irish and fought with them. And when he had put them to flight, Arthur with his men went forward to the ship, carrying away the cauldron full of Irish money. And he disembarked at the house of Llwydden the son of Kelcoed, at Porth Kerddin in Dyved. And there is the measure of the cauldron.

Then Arthur summoned unto him all the warriors that were in the three Islands of Britain, and in the three Islands adjacent, and all that were in France and in Armorica, in Normandy and in the Summer Country, and all that were chosen footmen and valiant horsemen. And with all these he went into Ireland. And in Ireland there was great fear and terror concerning him. And when Arthur had landed in the country, there came unto him the saints of Ireland and besought his protection. And he granted his protection unto them, and they gave him their blessing. Then the men of Ireland came unto Arthur, and brought him provisions. And Arthur went as far as Esgeir Oervel in Ireland, to the place where the Boar Trwyth was with his seven young pigs. And the dogs were let loose upon him from all sides. That day until evening the Irish fought with him, nevertheless he laid waste the fifth part of Ireland. And on the day following the household of Arthur fought with him, and they were worsted by him and got no advantage. And the third day Arthur himself encountered him, and he fought with him nine nights and nine days without so much as killing even one little pig. The warriors inquired of Arthur what was the origin of that swine; and he told them that he was once a king, and that God had transformed him into a swine for his sins.

Then Arthur sent Gwrhyr Gwalstawt Ieithoedd, to endeavour to speak with him. And Gwrhyr assumed the form of a bird, and alighted upon the top of the lair, where he was with the seven young pigs. And Gwrhyr Gwalstawt Ieithoedd asked him, "By him who turned you into this form, if you can speak, let some one of you, I beseech you, come and talk with Arthur." Grugyn Gwrych Ereint made answer to him. (Now his bristles were like silver wire, and whether he went through the wood or through the plain, he was to be traced by the glittering of his bristles.) And this was the answer that Grugyn made, "By him who turned us into this form, we will not do so, and we will not speak with Arthur. That we have been transformed thus is enough for us to suffer, without your coming here to fight with us."

"I will tell you. Arthur comes but to fight for the comb, and the razor, and the scissors, which are between the two ears of Twrch Trwyth."

Said Grugyn, "Except he first take his life, he will never have those precious things. And to-morrow morning we will rise up hence, and we will go into Arthur's country, and there will we do all the mischief that we can."

So they set forth through the sea towards Wales. And Arthur and his hosts, and his horses and his dogs, entered Prydwen, that they might encounter them without delay. Twrch Trwyth landed in Porth Cleis in Dyved, and Arthur came to Mynyw. The next day it was told to Arthur that they had gone by, and he overtook them as they were killing the cattle of Kynnwas Kwrr y Vagyl, having slain all that were at Aber Gleddyf, of man and beast, before the coming of Arthur.

Now when Arthur approached, Twrch Trwyth went on as far as Preseleu, and Arthur and his hosts followed him thither, and Arthur sent men to hunt him; Eli and Trachmyr, leading Drutwyn the whelp of Greid the son of Eri, and Gwarthegyd the son of Kaw, in another quarter, with the two dogs of Glythmyr Ledewig, and Bedwyr leading Cavall, Arthur's own dog. And all the warriors ranged themselves around the Nyver. And there came there the three sons of Cleddyf Divwlch, men who had gained much fame at the slaying of Yskithyrwyn Penbaedd; and they went on from Glyn Nyver, and came to Cwm Kerwyn.

And there Twrch Trwyth made a stand, and slew four of Arthur's champions, Gwarthegyd the son of Kaw, and Tarawc of Allt Clwyd, and Rheidwn the son of Eli Atver, and Iscovan Hael. And after he had slain these men, he made a second stand in the same place. And there he slew Gwydre the son of Arthur, and Garselit Wyddel, and Glew the son of Ysgawd, and Iscawyn the son of Panon; and there he himself was wounded.

And the next morning before it was day, some of the men came up with him. And he slew Huandaw, and Gogigwr, and Penpingon, three attendants upon Glewlwyd

Gavaelvawr, so that Heaven knows, he had not an attendant remaining, excepting only Llaesgevyn, a man from whom no one ever derived any good. And together with these, he slew many of the men of that country, and Gwlydyn Saer, Arthur's chief Architect.

Then Arthur overtook him at Pelumyawc, and there he slew Madawc the son of Teithyon, and Gwyn the son of Tringad, the son of Neved, and Eiryawn Penllorau. Thence he went to Aberteivi, where he made another stand, and where he slew Kyflas the son of Kynan, and Gwilenhin king of France. Then he went as far as Glyn Ystu, and there the men and the dogs lost him.

Then Arthur summoned unto him Gwyn ab Nudd, and he asked him if he knew aught of Twrch Trwyth. And he said that he did not.

And all the huntsmen went to hunt the swine as far as Dyffryn Llychwr. And Grugyn Gwallt Ereint, and Llwydawg Govynnyad closed with them and killed all the huntsmen, so that there escaped but one man only. And Arthur and his hosts came to the place where Grugyn and Llwydawg were. And there he let loose the whole of the dogs upon them, and with the shout and barking that was set up, Twrch Trwyth came to their assistance.

And from the time that they came across the Irish sea, Arthur had never got sight of him until then. So he set men and dogs upon him, and thereupon he started off and went to Mynydd Amanw. And there one of his young pigs was killed. Then they set upon him life for life, and Twrch Llawin was slain, and then there was slain another of the swine, Gwys was his name. After that he went on to Dyffryn Amanw, and there Banw and Bennwig were killed. Of all his pigs there went with him alive from that place none save Grugyn Gwallt Ereint, and Llwydawg Govynnyad.

Thence he went on to Llwch Ewin, and Arthur overtook him there, and he made a stand. And there he slew Echel Forddwytwll, and Garwyli the son of Gwyddawg Gwyr, and

many men and dogs likewise. And thence they went to
Llwch Tawy. Grugyn Gwrych Ereint parted from them
there, and went to Din Tywi. And thence he proceeded to
Ceredigiawn, and Eli and Trachmyr with him, and a
multitude likewise. Then he came to Garth Gregyn, and
there Llwydawg Govynnyad fought in the midst of them,
and slew Rhudvyw Rhys and many others with him. Then
Llwydawg went thence to Ystrad Yw, and there the men of
Armorica met him, and there he slew Hirpeissawg the king
of Armorica, and Llygatrudd Emys, and Gwrbothu,
Arthur's uncles, his mother's brothers, and there was he
himself slain.

Twrch Trwyth went from there to between Tawy and Euyas,
and Arthur summoned all Cornwall and Devon unto him,
to the estuary of the Severn, and he said to the warriors of
this Island, "Twrch Trwyth has slain many of my men, but,
by the valour of warriors, while I live he shall not go into
Cornwall. And I will not follow him any longer, but I will
oppose him life to life. Do ye as ye will." And he resolved
that he would send a body of knights, with the dogs of the
Island, as far as Euyas, who should return thence to the
Severn, and that tried warriors should traverse the Island,
and force him into the Severn. And Mabon the son of
Modron, came up with him at the Severn, upon Gwynn
Mygddon, the horse of Gweddw, and Goreu the son of
Custennin, and Menw the son of Teirgwaedd; this was
betwixt Llyn Lliwan and Aber Gwy. And Arthur fell upon
him together with the champions of Britain. And Osla
Kyllellvawr drew near, and Manawyddan the son of Llyr,
and Kacmwri the servant of Arthur, and Gwyngelli, and
they seized hold of him, catching him first by his feet, and
plunged him in the Severn, so that it overwhelmed him. On
the one side, Mabon the son of Modron spurred his steed
and snatched his razor from him, and Kyledyr Wyllt came
up with him on the other side, upon another steed, in the

Severn, and took from him the scissors. But before they could obtain the comb, he had regained the ground with his feet, and from the moment that he reached the shore, neither dog, nor man, nor horse could overtake him until he came to Cornwall. If they had had trouble in getting the jewels from him, much more had they in seeking to save the two men from being drowned. Kacmwri, as they drew him forth, was dragged by two millstones into the deep. And as Osla Kyllellvawr was running after the boar, his knife had dropped out of the sheath, and he had lost it, and after that, the sheath became full of water, and its weight drew him down into the deep, as they were drawing him forth.

Then Arthur and his hosts proceeded until they overtook the boar in Cornwall, and the trouble which they had met with before was mere play to what they encountered in seeking the comb. But from one difficulty to another, the comb was at length obtained. And then he was hunted from Cornwall, and driven straight forward into the deep sea. And thenceforth it was never known whither he went; and Aned and Aethlem with him. Then went Arthur to Gelliwic, in Cornwall, to anoint himself, and to rest from his fatigues.

Said Arthur, "Is there any one of the marvels yet unobtained?"

Said one of his men, "There is--the blood of the witch Orddu, the daughter of the witch Orwen, of Penn Nant Govid, on the confines of Hell." Arthur set forth towards the North, and came to the place where was the witch's cave. And Gwyn ab Nudd, and Gwythyr the son of Greidawl, counselled him to send Kacmwri, and Hygwyd his brother to fight with the witch. As they entered the cave, the witch seized upon them, and she caught Hygwyd by the hair of his head, and threw him on the floor beneath her. And Kacmwri caught her by the hair of her head, and dragged her to the earth from off Hygwyd, but she turned again upon them both, and drove them both out with kicks and with cuffs.

And Arthur was wroth at seeing his two attendants almost slain, and he sought to enter the cave; but Gwyn and Gwythyr said unto him, "It would not be fitting or seemly for us to see thee squabbling with a hag. Let Hiramreu and Hireidil go to the cave." So they went. But if great was the trouble of the first two that went, much greater was that of these two. And heaven knows that not one of the four could move from the spot, until they placed them all upon Llamrei, Arthur's mare. And then Arthur rushed to the door of the cave, and at the door he struck at the witch, with Carnwennan his dagger, and clove her in twain, so that she fell in two parts. And Kaw, of North Britain, took the blood of the witch and kept it.

Then Kilhwch set forward, and Goreu, the son of Custennin, with him, and as many as wished ill to Yspaddaden Penkawr. And they took the marvels with them to his court. And Kaw of North Britain came and shaved his beard, skin, and flesh clean off to the very bone from ear to ear.

"Art thou shaved, man?" said Kilhwch.

"I am shaved," answered he.

"Is thy daughter mine now?"

"She is thine," said he, "but therefor needest thou not thank me, but Arthur who hath accomplished this for thee. By my free will thou shouldest never have had her, for with her I lose my life." Then Goreu, the son of Custennin, seized him by the hair of his head, and dragged him after him to the keep, and cut off his head and placed it on a stake on the citadel. Then they took possession of his castle, and of his treasures.

And that night Olwen became Kilhwch's bride, and she continued to be his wife as long as she lived. And the hosts of Arthur dispersed themselves, each man to his own country. And thus did Kilhwch obtain Olwen, the daughter of Yspaddaden Penkawr.

More Arthurian Legends

We'd love for you to join our community! For more Arthurian texts, resources, and fiction, visit some of the links below!

The Website
www.mythbank.com

Facebook
www.facebook.com/mythbank

Instagram
instagram.com/mythbankwebsite

Printed in Great Britain
by Amazon